Published in 1997 by Modern Publishing,
A Division of Unisystems, Inc.

Characters Copyright © 1997 Tony Hutchings.
Happy Ending Book™ Tony Hutchings.

®-Honey Bear Books is a trademark owned by
Honey Bear Productions, Inc., and is registered
in the U.S. Patent and Trademark Office.

Printed in China.

A HAPPY ENDING BOOK™

The New Baby

illustrated by Tony Hutchings

MODERN PUBLISHING
A Division of Unisystems, Inc.
New York, New York 10022

Tippu and Monty were playing games in the garden, racing and shouting. Then Mommy came out with Tippu's new baby sister. "Pipe down!" cried Mommy. "You'll wake the baby!" Tippu scowled. "The baby spoils everything," he muttered. "You can't have any fun with a new baby around."

That night, Tippu asked Mommy where they were going to go on the first day of his school vacation. They always went somewhere special. "We can't go anywhere this year," Mommy said. "You know we can't leave the baby alone."

On Saturday, Monty brought his little sister to the playground!

"Can't you take her home?" asked Tippu. "Then we could have some real fun."

"Of course not," said Monty. "Besides, I like her."

"Suit yourself," said Tippu crossly. "My baby sister is just a pain in the neck. I'll never like her."

"Yes you will," said Monty. "Just you wait!"

But Tippu refused to play with Monty and his sister.

Tippu always went roller-skating with Daddy on Saturday afternoons. "That baby can't spoil my day with Daddy," thought Tippu.

But Daddy said, "Sorry, Tippu. Not today. Your Great Aunt Lucy is coming with a present for your baby sister. "

Great Aunt Lucy arrived with an armful of presents. "I can't wait to see the new baby!" she cried. "She must be beautiful!"

"She is!" said Daddy. Mommy beamed.

"But first, where is my Tippu?" asked Great Aunt Lucy. "I want to see him first. I have a present for him!" But Tippu was not in the house.

"We'd better look for him," said Great Aunt Lucy.

Daddy looked all over, outside and inside. But Tippu was nowhere to be found.

Mommy began to look worried. "Where can he be?" she asked. "Why is he hiding from us?"

"Perhaps nobody has been making a fuss over him since the new baby came," suggested Great Aunt Lucy.

Mommy's eyes filled with tears.

Suddenly there was a cry from the baby upstairs. "Don't worry," Daddy said. "I'll quiet her." But what did Daddy see when he opened the baby's door?

There was Tippu! "Stop crying," Tippu was saying. "I'll take care of you." Tippu smiled as his little sister stopped crying. "I guess I could like you after all," Daddy heard Tippu say.

Daddy tiptoed downstairs, where
Mommy and Great Aunt Lucy were
searching for Tippu. "He's upstairs,"
Daddy whispered, "playing with the
baby!" Mommy clapped her hands
joyfully. "I'll go get him! I was so afraid
we'd lost our precious Tippu!"

Upstairs, Tippu looked pleased. "Mommy!" he cried. "She went to sleep!" Mommy hugged and kissed him. "Never mind the baby right now," she said. "My little boy matters too."

"I thought you loved the new baby more," Tippu whispered. "The new baby is so new and helpless, Tippu," said Mommy softly. "We love you more than ever." She hugged him.

Downstairs, after the presents were opened, Great Aunt Lucy said, "What a lucky baby she is, to have a brother like you."

"I suppose she is!" said Tippu.